K'tonton's
Sukkot
Adventure

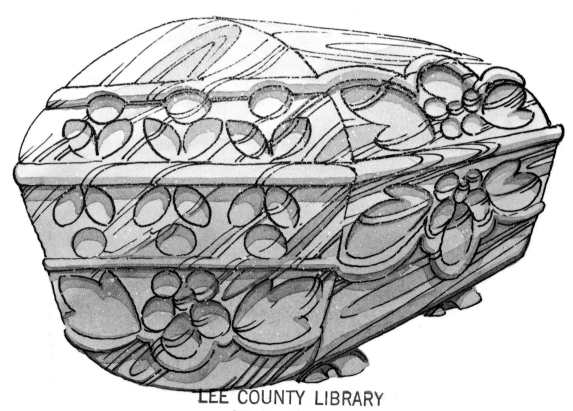

LEE COUNTY LIBRARY
107 Hawkins Ave.
Sanford, N. C. 27330

K'tonton's

Sukkot

The Jewish Publication Society

Philadelphia and Jerusalem

5753 / 1993

Adventure

Sadie Rose Weilerstein

illustrated by Joe Boddy

Text copyright 1993 by Sadie Rose Weilerstein

Illustrations copyright 1993 by Joe Boddy

Jacket illustration copyright 1993 by Joe Boddy

First edition. All rights reserved.

Manufactured in the United States of America

Printed on acid-free paper

Library of Congress Cataloging-in-Publication Data

Weilerstein, Sadie Rose, 1894–

K'tonton's Sukkot adventure / by Sadie Rose Weilerstein ;

illustrated by Joe Boddy.

p.   cm.

Summary: A small thumb-sized boy is born to aging Jewish parents
and has an adventure at the synagogue during the holiday of Sukkot.

ISBN 0–8276–0502–1

[1. Jews—Fiction. 2. Sukkot—Fiction.] I. Boddy, Joe, ill. II. title.

PZ7.W435Kv   1993   93–2990

[E]—dc20   CIP

                                             AC

10   9   8   7   6   5   4   3   2   1

Jacket and text design by Joanna Hill

Typeset in Century Schoolbook

Printed by Horowitz-Rae Printing Company

This book is dedicated with much love and thankfulness

to my great-grandsons

ALEX, SIMON, and NATAN

and to my great-granddaughters

HANNAH RIVKA and HANNAH SARAH.

May they be blessed.

Once upon a time there lived a husband and a wife. They had everything in the world to make them happy, or almost everything: a good snug house, clothes to keep them warm, challah, wine and fish for Friday night, and a special pudding—a kugel—every Sabbath. Only one thing was missing, and that was a child.

LEE COUNTY LIBRARY
107 Hawkins Ave.
Sanford, N. C. 27330

"Ah," the woman would sigh, "if only I could have a child! I shouldn't mind if he were no bigger than a thumb."

One day—it was on Sukkot, the Feast of Tabernacles—she was praying in the synagogue, when she happened to look down. There at her side stood a little old woman with deep, kind eyes, peering up at her from under a shawl.

"Why do you look so sad," asked the wrinkled old woman, "and why do you pray so earnestly?"

"I am sad," answered the wife, "because I have no child. Ah, that I might have a child! I shouldn't mind if he were no bigger than a thumb."

"In that case," said the little old woman, "I shall tell you what to do. Has your husband an etrog?"

"Indeed he has an etrog," said the wife, "a perfect, sweet-smelling citron that comes all the way from Israel."

"Then," said the old woman, "on the last day of Sukkot you must take the etrog and bite off the end, and you shall have your wish."

The wife thanked the little old woman kindly. When the last day of Sukkot came, she bit off the end of the etrog, just as she had been told.

Sure enough, before the year had passed, a little baby was born to her, a dear little boy baby, with black eyes and black hair, dimples in his knees, and thumbs just right for sucking. There was only one thing odd about him. He was exactly the size of a thumb, not one bit smaller or larger.

The wife laughed when she saw him. I don't know whether she laughed because she was so glad, or because it seemed so funny to have a baby as big as a thumb. Whichever it was, the husband said, "We shall call him Isaac, because Isaac in Hebrew means laughter."

Then, because they were so thankful to God for sending him, they gave the baby a second name, Samuel. But, of course, they couldn't call such a little baby, a baby no bigger than a thumb, Isaac Samuel all the time. So for everyday they called him K'tonton, which means very, very little; and that's exactly what he was.

The first thing they had to do was to find a cradle for the baby to sleep in.

"Fetch me the etrog box," the wife said to her husband. "It was the etrog box that brought my precious K'tonton, and the etrog box shall be his cradle."

The first thing they had to do was to find a
cradle for the baby to sleep in.

"Fetch me the etrog box," the wife said to her
husband. "It was the etrog box that brought my
precious K'tonton, and the etrog box shall be his
cradle."

She lifted the curving, rounded cover of the box.
When she turned it over, it rocked gently to and fro.
Then she took the flax that the etrog had been wrapped
in and spun it and wove it into softest linen. Out of the
linen she made a coverlet and sheet. Wherever she
went and whatever she did, little K'tonton in his little
cradle went with her.

LEE COUNTY LIBRARY
107 Hawkins Ave.
Sanford, N. C. 27330

Over the years K'tonton grew until he was as tall as his father's middle finger. When his mother cooked and baked for the holidays, he was a busy little chatterbox, dancing about on the table, peeping into the cinnamon box, hiding behind the sugar bowl, asking a question, so many questions, that at last his mother would say, "Blessings on your little head, K'tonton! If you don't let me keep my mind on my work, I'll be putting salt in the cake and sugar in the fish."

LEE COUNTY LIBRARY
107 Hawkins Ave.
Sanford, N. C. 27330

One year, when Sukkot came again, K'tonton saw his father place the etrog carefully into its box, ready to be carried to the synagogue.

"May I go with you, Father?" K'tonton asked.

"Wait until you're a little bigger," said Father. "Next year will be time enough."

But K'tonton did not want to wait until next year. He wanted to go now, this very day. What do you suppose he did? When his father wasn't looking, he climbed inside the etrog box and hid beneath the flax.

Soon the box was lifted. It was being carried through the streets.

Now they were in the synagogue; K'tonton could tell by the sound of the prayers. For a while he sat listening to the voice of the cantor.

Then he rose cautiously on tiptoe, pushed up the cover of the box, and peeked out. There wasn't a thing he could see! A high wooden bench rose like a wall before him.

I'll have to get up higher," thought K'tonton.

He looked about for something tall that he might climb. Ah! There was a lulav, a palm branch, leaning against the bench. It rose up straight and green and tall.

K'tonton grasped it with both hands and began climbing. It was easy at first; the braided holder supported his feet. But once he had passed the willow and the myrtle twigs, climbing became hard and slippery.

Up, up, he went, holding fast to the branch,
higher than the bench tops, higher than the heads
of the people.

Now at last he could see the synagogue. How beautiful it was! He had never dreamed a place could be so large. And so many men all wrapped in their tallitot, their long fringed prayer shawls.

But most beautiful of all was
the aron kodesh, the Holy Ark. On
its crimson curtains, flowers and
pomegranates and golden lions were
embroidered. K'tonton knew that
behind those curtains were the Sifrei
Torah, the scrolls of the Holy Law. His
heart filled with awe just to think of it.

Suddenly, the lulav, to which K'tonton clung, shook and rose into the air!

K'tonton held on tight to keep from tumbling and looked down.

His father had risen and taken the lulav in his hand. All about him rose other men with their lulavim.

The synagogue was like a forest of palm branches. They trembled and swayed; and K'tonton, clinging tightly to his father's lulav, swayed with them.

Oh, what a swinging and a swaying it was! East and west, north and south, up toward heaven, down toward earth.

"Hodu l'Adonai ki tov," sang the people. "Praise the Lord, for He is good."

Again the branches swayed. East and west, north and south, up toward heaven, down toward earth. K'tonton, swinging on the lulav, forgot that he had run away, forgot that he was supposed to be hiding.

"Hodu l'Adonai ki tov!" he sang. His shrill, high treble rose above the voices of the people.

In a moment every eye in the synagogue was on him. Men whispered and pointed. Women in the gallery crowded close to the railing. Even the cantor looked straight toward him.

As for K'tonton's father, he gasped in astonishment.

"K'tonton, you might have fallen and been hurt!" cried his father, as he snatched the little fellow from the lulav. "How do you come to be here at all?"

Soberly, K'tonton told the story of his adventure.

"If I were a proper parent, I would spank you," said his father. But K'tonton could see by the twinkle in his father's eye that the rod would be spared.

LEE COUNTY LIBRARY
107 Hawkins Ave.
Sanford, N. C. 27330

So, K'tonton stayed in the synagogue to join in the Hoshanot prayers and march in the procession of the palms.

Peering over the heads in front of her, a wrinkled little old woman with deep, kind eyes smiled and nodded.

"A wonder child," she murmured. "Even when he runs away, where does he run to? The synagogue!"

Glossary

Aron kodesh—the "Holy Ark" or cabinet containing the scrolls of the Torah.

Etrog—a yellow fruit smilar to a lemon, the citron is one of "four species" used on Sukkot. Willow, myrtle, and palm branch are the other three. The etrog is often carried in a special box lined with flax.

"Hodu l'Adonai ki tov"—the phrase "Praise the Lord, for He is good" from the Psalms, repeated as the lulav is waved on Sukkot and on Hoshanah Rabbah.

Hoshanot—a special procession during which people, carrying the lulav and etrog around the sanctuary, chant praises to God.

Kugel—a special vegetable or noodle pudding often served at Sabbath or festival meals.

Lulav—a palm branch, flanked by willow and myrtle branches, bound together with a special braided straw sheath. The tall, unopened branch, one of the "four species" used on Sukkot, is waved in six directions during the Sukkot service as well as in the sukkah (booth) to symbolize God's presence throughout the world.

Sifrei Torah—the books or scrolls of the Torah.

Sukkot—the Feast of Tabernacles, a holiday celebrating the fall harvest and commemorating the booths in which the Israelites dwelled when they wandered through the desert on their way to the Promised Land.

tallit (plural, **tallito**t)—a prayer shawl with fringes on its four corners, worn during most Jewish services.

Talmud—the Oral Law, a commentary on the Written Law (the Bible), which many Jews study daily throughout their lives.